Test #7675
R.L. 4.3
PTS. 3.0

JUST TELL ME
WHEN WE'RE
DEAD!

JUST TELL ME WHEN WE'RE DEAD!

Eth Clifford

Illustrated by George Hughes

Houghton Mifflin Company
Boston

Library of Congress Cataloging in Publication Data

Clifford, Eth, 1915–
  Just tell me when we're dead!

  Summary: Two sisters and the runaway cousin for whom
they are searching on an island find themselves in an
unexpected adventure.
  [1. Cousins — Fiction.   2. Orphans — Fiction.
3. Runaways — Fiction.   4. Islands — Fiction]   I. Hughes,
George, ill.   II. Title.
PZ7.C62214Ju   1983   [Fic]   83-10865
ISBN 0-395-33071-8

Printed in the United States of America

Q   10   9   8   7   6   5   4   3

Remembering warm and happy times—
this book is for

Martha and Amiel
Rita and Paul
Ethel and Maury

Contents

Contents

JUST TELL ME WHEN WE'RE DEAD!

•1•
The Voice
Inside

"I'm not going anyplace," nine-year-old Jeffrey Post said stubbornly. Anger made his dark eyes turn midnight black, so that the pupils seemed to disappear. A fisherman's cap, with the word *Captain* printed on it, was jammed down tight on his head, completely hiding his thick black hair. "I'm going to stay right here, and that's it."

He folded his arms and scowled at his grandmother. Then he glared at his Uncle Harry, sitting beside Grandmother Post on the sofa, and at Uncle Harry's two daughters, Mary Rose and Jo-Beth.

Grandmother Post hunched her shoulders and gave Harry Onetree a knowing glance. Harry Onetree sighed and rubbed his hand across the back of his neck.

"I'm getting tired of having you drag your feet whenever you have to stay with us, Jeff," he said. "You're not going to the end of the world, you know."

The two girls stared at their cousin with great interest.

Jo-Beth leaned toward her sister and whispered, "I thought Mommy said he would come quietly if we were here."

"What do you mean 'come quietly'?" Mary Rose hissed back. "You make it sound like we're police and he's a prisoner or something." Wouldn't you just know that Jo-Beth would start right in exaggerating everything, just because Jeff didn't want to stay with them while Grandmother Post went to the hospital, she thought.

Actually, Mrs. Onetree had said to her husband, "Harry, I can't leave the baby now, not while he's running a temperature. Why don't you take the girls with you? They'll have a nice friendly time with Jeffrey in the car. Maybe then he won't mind having to stay with us again for a while."

Grandmother Post and their cousin had moved to this small lake town two years ago, but it was the girls' first visit here, because usually Grandmother came to their house with Jeff.

"It's a sleepy kind of a place," their father had told them on the ride down. "They get some tourists in the summer, but now that it's fall, most of them are gone."

"That's all right," Mary Rose had assured her father. "I like nice quiet places."

The Post house was right on the lake, with just a small lawn in back that led to a private boat landing. Grandmother Post had decided at once that if they were to live near a lake, it was important for her grandson to know how to take care of himself around water. So Jeff had learned to swim and dive. And it wasn't long before he had his own rowboat, *The Sea Horse*, which he handled very well. He drew pictures of the tiny fish on each side of his boat.

Grandmother Post couldn't help worrying a little, even though Jeff was a fine swimmer. So there was one thing she insisted on: Whenever Jeff went out in *The Sea Horse*, he had to wear his life preserver — a bright-orange inflatable vest.

The girls had been rather excited when they finally arrived at the Post house after the long drive. They looked forward to having their nine-year-old cousin live with them for a while, because, as Jo-Beth had explained to Mary Rose on the trip, Jeff made things lively.

"Remember when Mom told Jeff his hair was so long he looked like a sheep dog?"

"And Jeff said he was going to let his hair grow until it was long enough to sit on," Mary Rose put in, giggling.

"Mom should have let him," Jo-Beth said, sounding regretful. "I wonder what that would have looked like."

"And then old Mrs. Hardcastle came by, selling raffle tickets, and she saw Jeff and said to Mom, 'I don't remember your having three little girls,' and Jeff got so mad he went rushing off to the barber without telling anyone."

"I don't know why that made him so mad," Jo-Beth said. "What's wrong with being a girl?"

"I don't want any trouble getting that young man to come back with us," Mr. Onetree said, interrupting their conversation. "I want you girls to persuade Jeff to come along with us without the usual fuss."

"Okay," they agreed.

But it wasn't okay, for it appeared now that they might have to leave without Jeff after all.

Mr. Onetree said, "Now, Jeff," in a firm voice. He was beginning to lose his temper.

Jeff just turned away and went to the window and stared out, standing like a sailor on duty, his back stiff and straight, not a muscle moving, his eyes fixed on the quiet water.

Mary Rose wished her father hadn't started his sentence with "Now, Jeff." Somehow whenever grown-ups started sentences that way, it meant they were going to tell you something you didn't want to hear. The words were supposed to make everything sound reasonable. Mary Rose could see that nothing was going to sound reasonable to Jeff. He just didn't want Grandmother Post to go to the hospital. He didn't want to come and stay with the Onetrees for a couple of months, even though Mary Rose, who was ten and a half, and Jo-Beth, who was seven and a half, would be right there too.

Mr. Onetree made up his mind. "Now, Jeff," he said again, "I know all of this seems very unfair to you, but that's the way things are sometimes, and there's nothing any of us can do about it. Mary Rose, I'm going to take Grandmother Post to the hospital now and get her settled in. I'm putting you in charge here because I know I can count on you."

Jo-Beth nodded. It certainly was true that her sister could be trusted, for Mary Rose was a sensible, dependable girl.

"Jeffrey's bag is all packed." Grandmother Post's eyes were dry, but her voice was husky and sad, as if she had a small waterfall of tears somewhere inside her.

"And Jeff can bring along his rock collection. And his ant colony and whatever else he wants to take along. Within reason," Mr. Onetree added.

"Aren't you going to kiss me good-bye?" Grandmother Post asked. Jeff didn't turn around, not even when his grandmother sighed. "I'll call you every chance I get," she said.

Mr. Onetree shook his head and took Grandmother Post by the arm. "He'll get over it once he's home with us," he whispered. Aloud, he told his daughter, "Remember, Mary Rose, we'll leave as soon as I get back. I want to try to make it back home before dark. Keep an eye on things here."

Grandmother Post stopped at the door and glanced back, a hurt look in her eyes. But Jeff remained at the window with his back to the room. Even after the door slammed behind the adults, he didn't move.

"Honestly!" Jo-Beth burst out as soon as her father and grandmother were gone. "That was real mean, Jeffrey Post. Suppose something happens in the hospital. Then how will you feel?"

"Be quiet." Mary Rose glared at her sister. "Nothing's going to happen. Everything's going to be all right," she insisted with a warning frown and shake of the head.

Now at last Jeffrey turned around. "Who cares, anyway?"

Even Mary Rose couldn't believe this. "You're talking about your very own grand-mother!"

Jeffrey gave her a blank look. His eyes seemed to have turned a deeper black. The fact that Jo-Beth could not see his pupils made her uncomfortable. Maybe that was why Jeff didn't feel things the way she and her sister did, Jo-Beth told herself. He was different somehow. *She* would never let anyone leave without a farewell squeeze, no matter what.

It was just an act, Mary Rose decided. Probably that was how boys thought they were supposed to behave.

With the grown-ups gone, the three children stood about awkwardly at first, not quite knowing what to do. But at a time like this, Mary Rose could be relied on to think of something.

"Would you like to have something to eat?" she asked the others politely.

"Sure," said Jo-Beth promptly. She was always hungry. "What can we have?"

"Let's go into the kitchen. Come on, Jeff. I'll make something nice."

From the fixed way Jeff was staring at her, Mary Rose could tell he wasn't looking at her at all. In fact, he didn't even seem to understand that Mary Rose was talking to him.

It was as if Jeff was listening to a voice inside, and listening very hard.

•2•
His Poor Broken Body
on the Rocks Below

"Well, do you or don't you, Jeff?" Jo-Beth was impatient. What was the matter with him, anyway, just standing there with that strange look on his face? "Want to eat, I mean."

She wondered if Jeff's eating habits had changed. The last time he stayed with them, when his father and mother had gone on one of their trips, Jeff wouldn't eat any vegetable that was green. So Mrs. Onetree cooked beets, which Jo-Beth hated, and squash, which her father wouldn't allow to be put on his plate.

Jeff finally answered: "I don't want anything to eat. I'm going upstairs to my room."

"Sure, you go ahead." Mary Rose gave him a little nod of understanding. "We'll be in the kitchen if you change your mind."

Jeff probably needed to be alone for a while, Mary Rose decided, just to sit in his room, in familiar surroundings. She could almost imagine Jeff sitting on his bed, looking around at all the things he loved.

As a matter of fact, this was exactly what Jeff was doing. His glance wandered from the locker at the foot of his bed — an old sea chest his grandmother had bought for him — to the blue-and-white pennant pinned on the wall above his desk. He had won that in his very first boat race. Right under the pennant was the genuine eagle feather he had found when he went camping.

His rock-polishing machine wasn't covered. Jeff frowned. He liked everything in his room to be neat and orderly. He got up and slipped the plastic sheet over it. Then, without thinking, he picked up a smooth green stone from his desk and began to rub it between his fingers. It was called a worry stone. Rubbing the stone was supposed to relax you.

Still holding the stone, he studied the huge poster over his bed. It was a picture of astronauts taking the first walk on the moon. Under the figures there were printed words: ONE SMALL STEP FOR MAN, ONE GIANT LEAP FOR MANKIND.

That's what Jeff would do someday. Maybe he would go beyond the moon, far beyond, into deep space. He would do it alone, too. Jeff Post didn't need anybody!

He looked at the words again: ONE SMALL STEP FOR MAN. It gave Jeff an idea. He put the worry stone down and went to his desk. He pulled a sheet of paper from one of the drawers, uncapped a pen and began to scribble on the page. He crumpled several sheets of paper, which he deposited carefully in the wastepaper basket, before he was satisfied at last with what he had written.

While Jeff was concentrating, touching the end of the pen to his lips from time to time, in the kitchen Jo-Beth was chatting sunnily as she opened a jar of peanut butter and spread a generous helping on some of Grandmother Post's homemade bread. "You'd think Jeff would want to come and stay with us." Jo-Beth was now busily slicing a banana and dropping it piece by piece on top of the peanut butter. "We'd be good for him," Jo-Beth added with a lofty air.

Mary Rose watched with tight lips as her sister slapped another slice of bread on top of the banana and then squashed the whole thing together until the food ran out on all sides.

"I hate the way you eat." Mary Rose was disgusted.

Jo-Beth didn't care. She enjoyed squashing different kinds of soft foods. She loved the way they dripped out of the bread. She liked licking her way around the edges before she took a good big bite.

She had finished her sandwich and her glass of milk and Mary Rose had cleaned up and put everything away when Jo-Beth said, "Don't you think it feels kind of extra quiet around here?"

Mrs. Onetree always grew suspicious if

their house was too quiet, especially if she couldn't hear the girls arguing or giggling. Mary Rose was suspicious now. She tilted her head, the way her mother usually did to hear if the baby was crying.

Jo-Beth tilted her head as well. "What do you suppose Jeff is doing so long in his room?"

Mary Rose didn't know, but she was certainly going to find out.

"Wait for me," Jo-Beth called as Mary Rose dashed out of the kitchen and began running upstairs.

"Jeff!" Mary Rose shouted, and pounded on the door. There was no reply. Mary Rose knocked again, then flung open the door. The room was empty.

It was Jo-Beth who spotted the large envelope leaning against the pillow on Jeff's bed.

"How did he get out?" Mary Rose was puzzled. If Jeff had come down the steps, the girls would have seen him from the kitchen.

"He's thrown himself from the window," Jo-Beth said, her eyes shining with excitement. "I just knew Jeff would do something awful."

"You did not!" Mary Rose snapped back.

But Jo-Beth paid no attention. She went on with gloomy satisfaction: "We'll probably find his poor broken body on the rocks below." She pointed to the bed. "Look, he's left a suicide note for us."

"You're doing it again." Mary Rose couldn't help being irritated.

The sisters looked very much alike, with their fine straight brown hair and dark-brown eyes, except, of course, for those times Mary Rose had to wear an eye patch over her right eye to make her "lazy" left eye work. Mr. Onetree had once remarked that the black eye patch made Mary Rose look like a small angry pirate who'd lost her treasure map.

The girls looked alike, but they were very different. Mary Rose never jumped to conclusions. She liked to figure things out before she made up her mind about what might be going on. Jo-Beth, on the other hand, was always play-acting.

"Nine-year-old boys don't commit suicide," Mary Rose said in her no-nonsense way. She walked to the bed, picked up the envelope, then went to the window and peered out. "He must have climbed out on the roof and across that big branch and then down the tree," she decided.

"Can you see his body?"

"No. And there are no rocks down there, either." Mary Rose tapped the envelope against her chin thoughtfully.

"Please, Mary Rose. Read the letter. I can't stand not knowing." Jo-Beth gave a small shiver of delight. How mysterious it all was. Jeff missing, and a letter left behind with who knew what kind of message.

Mary Rose tore the envelope open so slowly and carefully that it made Jo-Beth want to snatch it from her. If that wasn't just like her sister! It was the way she opened birthday presents and Christmas presents, to keep from tearing the wrapping paper. And then, of course, Mary Rose saved the paper. She had heaps of wrapping paper in a box on the shelf in her closet.

"Just tear it! You can't save the envelope for anything!"

Mary Rose didn't reply. She was reading the note.

"Well, what does it say?"

Mary Rose handed the sheet to her sister. Jo-Beth read it aloud:

Don't try to find me am going west, far west. Jo Beth can have my ant colony and Mary Rose can have my rock collection. If I don't ever come back.

Jeff

P.S. Nobody has to worry, I know how to take care of myself.

Jo-Beth turned the letter round and round in her fingers. "I'd rather have the rock collection," she said honestly. "Do you want to swap with me?"

Mary Rose ignored her sister. She was thinking how angry her father would be when he returned from the hospital. She could just hear him: "I left you in charge, Mary Rose!"

She turned and looked out the window again.

Jo-Beth, as if reading her sister's thoughts, said knowingly, "Daddy is going to be awfully mad at you." And not at me, Jo-Beth told herself, because I'm only seven and a half.

"He didn't go west," Mary Rose said suddenly, staring down at the boat landing. "I bet he didn't get very far. Come on. We're going to go look for him."

"Where?"

"I think I have an idea." Mary Rose rushed out of the room and down the stairs without looking back to see if Jo-Beth was following.

•3•
You Can't Go West
in a Rowboat

"I knew it," Mary Rose said. "*The Sea Horse* is gone."

"You can't go west in a rowboat," Jo-Beth objected. "Can you?" she asked uncertainly.

"Don't be ridiculous." Mary Rose shaded her eyes from the sun and glanced across the lake to what seemed like an oasis of trees some distance away in the water. "I bet he went to the island."

"The island?" Jo-Beth narrowed her eyes and peered hard. "But it's closed."

"You can't close an island." Mary Rose knew what her sister meant, however. Mr. Onetree had told the girls about the island on the trip down. There was a park and picnic grounds and maybe some rides for children. Mr. Onetree wasn't sure about that, because he had never been there. In the summer, when tourists arrived, a ferry boat made regular trips back and forth.

"Can we go see it?" Jo-Beth had asked eagerly.

Her father had shaken his head. "They close up after Labor Day, once the kids are back in school. Anyway, there wouldn't be time. We're just here to get Grandma to the hospital and pick up Jeff."

"What are we going to do now?" Jo-Beth knew her sister was planning something, because she was pulling at her lower lip with her thumb and forefinger. When Mary Rose started folding her lip that way, some kind of action always followed.

"We're going to the island to look for him."

Jo-Beth looked around. "How?" she demanded. "The ferry isn't running. We can't swim there. Mary Rose! We're not, are we?"

Jo-Beth was immediately fascinated by the picture that sprang to her mind. There they were, the two of them, swimming and swimming, the island seeming to shimmer away from them each time they came closer to it. And Jo-Beth, getting very tired, beginning to sink, saying bravely, "You go on, Mary Rose. You must save our cousin."

How sad everyone would be when she was gone. They would touch their eyes with damp handkerchiefs and sob, "She was so good, so . . . "

Mary Rose shook her rudely out of her daydream. "Come on. We're going down to the ferry." They had passed it in the car on their way to Grandmother Post's house. "I saw some rowboats there."

Mary Rose took off briskly across the backyards. Jo-Beth could hardly keep up with her. And because Jo-Beth was glancing down at the different boat landings, it was she who found what they needed in the water behind a large old-fashioned house.

She stopped short. "Mary Rose. Look!"

Mary Rose turned around, annoyed. "We can't wait . . . " She broke off as she followed her sister's pointing finger, then came running back. "A rowboat would be faster," she began.

Jo-Beth interrupted: "But suppose the rowboats are all tied up for the winter? This one is just sort of floating free."

What the girls were staring at was a small boat, carved in the shape of a swan, with two wooden seats and pedals at the bottom that had to be worked up and down to make the boat go.

Mary Rose looked back at the house. "I guess I better ask if we can take it."

"There isn't time. We have to find Jeff before Daddy gets back."

"I'm steering," Mary Rose said firmly.

"I saw it first."

"Never *mind*. Just get in. You can steer it on the way back."

As the girls pumped the pedals up and down and Mary Rose aimed for the island, Jo-Beth began to imagine all kinds of adventures waiting for them. A deserted island. They would have to find food somehow. Mary Rose would be afraid to climb the trees, but Jo-Beth would go right up and throw coconuts down. They would build a shelter from branches and leaves, and Jo-Beth would make grass skirts . . .

"Camels," Jo-Beth said aloud, softly.

One camel would be waiting just for her. He would turn his large brown eyes toward her and sink to the ground. She would clamber up and sit between his two humps. Then the two of them would go slowly, with dignity, around the island . . .

Mary Rose, glancing at her sister, realized that she was daydreaming again. I wish I could just drift off like she does, Mary Rose thought with envy. But even if she could, Mary Rose decided, this would be the wrong time. She had to figure out just how they would go about finding Jeff on the island. She was sure he wouldn't answer if the girls shouted his name. Jeff could be so exasperating at times.

Maybe they ought to split up, with Mary Rose going one way and Jo-Beth going the other. After all, it couldn't be a very big island. No, they had better stay together. If anything happened to Jo-Beth, and with Jeff missing, her father would never talk to Mary Rose again.

Jo-Beth snapped out of her daydream. Her legs were beginning to get tired pumping up and down. "I think Jeff was dumb to run away like this. I wonder why he did."

"Just pedal," Mary Rose replied shortly. "Let's just get there."

But she couldn't help wondering too. What was it Jeff had been thinking about in his room that had made him climb out the window and take off in *The Sea Horse?*

•4•
The Man with the Yellow Tiger Eyes

Jeff had started off thinking about grown-ups. You couldn't trust them, he told himself as he paced back and forth in his room.

When they moved into this house, Jeff's grandmother had promised that they would never move again. This was where he would grow up, with his grandmother to take care of him. And now she was gone. She said she was coming back. But that was what his parents had said.

"We'll come back," they had told him each time they planned a trip.

"Why can't you take me with you?"

There was always a reason why he had to stay behind. First he had been too small, too young. Then they hadn't wanted to take him out of school. And then they had insisted he would have more fun at summer camp or visiting with his cousins because he would be with people his own age.

"You can come along with us when you're bigger," his father had told him.

"How much bigger?"

"When you're twelve," his father promised. "I give you my word, Jeff."

"Meanwhile," his mother added with a warm smile, "we'll bring you something extra special when we come home."

Each time they left, Jeff would stand and watch them go, with a hard lump in his throat that he couldn't swallow. No matter how often they went away, he couldn't get used to the flood of sadness inside.

The last time they went away, they didn't come back. They were never coming back again. His grandmother had expected him to cry. But why should he cry?

So what if they weren't coming back? When were they ever around, anyway? Where were they when all the other parents came to school on parents' day? Where were they when he put his tooth under his pillow? Where were they when he won the skateboard contest?

"So what?" Jeff shouted at his grandmother. "Who cares?"

That was the worst thing they had ever done to him. He would never forgive them. Never.

"I hate them," he had said in a furious voice. Then he fled the room, tore up the stairs and slammed his door shut.

And now it was his grandmother who was leaving. She wouldn't come back either, no matter what she said. She was old. She was fifty-two. That was more than half a century!

When he had come upstairs a little while ago to get away from Mary Rose and Jo-Beth, he had wished he could stow away on a spaceship. He couldn't do that, but he knew what he could do. He could go hide out on the island. He wouldn't stay there for very long. Later on he probably would go out west. He'd ride the wild horses no one else could ride. People would whisper about him and call him "the mysterious stranger who never smiled," and no one would know his secret.

Meanwhile, though, he had better get over to the island right away. Having made up his mind, he wrote a note and left it propped against his pillow. Then, with one last look at his room, Jeff went out the window because, with the girls in the kitchen, he couldn't sneak out the back door. His cousins would have asked a million questions, and Mary Rose would probably have tried to stop him. She had kind of a bossy air.

Once Jeff was safely down, he had no trouble getting away quietly in *The Sea Horse*.

Jeff knew the island well. The most direct route was straight across the lake to the swan-pedal-boat landing. But Jeff intended to stay hidden. So, although it was the long way around, he rowed past the ferry slip and a number of other inlets until he reached the caretaker's small boat landing.

It wouldn't do to leave *The Sea Horse* where it could be seen. Pulling his boat ashore was hard work, but Jeff finally managed to beach it. Once ashore, it was easy to cover the boat with branches so that it wasn't visible. Even if old Hugo Axel came by, as the caretaker did about once every couple of weeks, he wouldn't notice.

Jeff grinned. Now he really was on his own. Nobody was going to bother him on this quiet, peaceful island.

A dirt path led from a cottage past a grove of trees and then twisted its way to the picnic grounds and the playground. Whistling softly, Jeff began to walk along the path. He stopped once to examine a line of ants busily carrying bits of leaves back to an anthill. The bits of leaves were so much larger than the tiny ants that it seemed as if the leaves were doing the walking.

Ants weren't ever alone, Jeff thought. If one ant died, there was always another to take its place.

As he walked on again, his mind was so busy with thoughts about the ants that he had almost reached the grove when the sound of voices shocked him into dropping quickly to the ground.

Had a search party come looking for him this fast?

Jeff squirmed along the ground quietly until he came to a small hill that overlooked the grove. Slowly he inched his way up the hill until he was able to peer over the rim.

Two men were standing below and arguing. One was tall and thin, with a gritty voice and gray wispy hair that he kept pushing impatiently back from his knobby forehead. The other man, who had two pieces of rope coiled around his arm, was short and square-shaped. He looked as if someone had drawn a few boxes and then added a head and legs and arms. His face didn't seem to belong to his body. When he spoke, two long front teeth were visible. His mustache sprang away on each side of his upper lip, like wire whiskers. His brown eyes peered from above a twitching, rabbitlike nose.

"You told me," he was saying as Jeff stared down from the hill, "that all we had to do was come here and we would see these two giant rocks. Right? One someplace over here and one someplace over there. And then all we would have to do is lay out the ropes from the rocks until the ends meet. And where the two ends meet, they'd be pointing to the exact tree where you buried the money. Stop me if I'm wrong, Fingers. Then we dig and — bingo! — there it is! Right?"

"Right."

"Sure. Right. So tell me, where are the rocks?"

"Lippy, I tell you there were two big rocks here. I was in jail, meathead. How should I know somebody would start moving rocks? What's the difference? It's got to be one of those two trees over there, standing together. If we don't find the money under one of them, it'll be under the other."

The tall, thin man had been glancing around casually as he spoke. He let his gaze travel up, then he stiffened and looked puzzled. He thought he had seen a flash of something orange. "Hey, Lippy, did you see something move up there?"

Lippy shrugged. "Maybe you saw an animal."

An orange animal? Fingers nudged his partner. "Keep talking," he said in a low voice. "I think I'll take a look."

Jeff made a face. In his hurry to cover *The Sea Horse,* he'd forgotten to remove his orange life preserver.

I'd better get out of here fast, he decided.

He rose so quickly that he slipped and went rolling down the hill. At the bottom he was about to leap to his feet when he felt his arm caught and held in a firm grip.

He looked up and gasped. The tall, thin man was staring down at him through narrowed yellow tiger eyes. He was smiling, a smile that promised that a lot of unpleasant things were about to happen.

"Going someplace, kid?" the thin man asked.

•5•
Danger!
Stay Out!

When the thin man dragged Jeff to where Lippy was waiting, Lippy's nose twitched and his mustache quivered so hard that Jeff couldn't help staring.

"You think he heard what we said? What'll we do with him?" Lippy asked in a shrill voice.

Fingers shook Jeff. "Who else is here? And don't lie to me, kid. I can spot a lie in a minute."

"A whole bunch of us," Jeff told him promptly. "My whole boy scout troop." He was thinking quickly, making things up as he talked. "We're here on an overnight hike. The scoutmaster and everybody. They'll all be here any minute, so you better get out of here while you can."

The two men listened hard. There were no voices, no tramping feet, no coughs, no sign of people approaching. The silence of the island was broken only by bird calls and the soft rustling of leaves scurried along the ground by the breeze.

"I don't hear no boy scouts," Lippy said. "He's lying."

Fingers grabbed Jeff's arm and pinched it cruelly. His yellow tiger eyes glittered with such mean anger that Jeff stopped trying to get his arm free.

Lippy recognized that look with alarm. "Hey, Fingers. No rough stuff. You said we'd dig up the money and there wouldn't be no rough stuff, no matter what."

"This kid is trouble. Big trouble. We gotta get rid of him."

"You can let me go." Jeff tried to keep his voice steady. "I won't tell anybody what you were doing."

Lippy glanced about desperately. He had to stop Fingers. Stealing was one thing, but what Fingers had in mind . . . He shuddered. If they could just get the kid out of the way until they found the money and got off the island . . . It was then that Lippy spotted a small brick building in the distance. His face brightened.

"Hey, Fingers. Look! Why don't we just stick the kid in there?"

Fingers shook his head stubbornly.

"I'm not a hatchet man," Lippy insisted.

"You telling *me* what to do?" Fingers flared.

"Just asking, that's all," Lippy said hastily.

"Okay. We'll do it your way. This time, Bring the rope we were going to measure with. March, kid."

Still holding Jeff's arm, Fingers began to move swiftly toward the building, forcing Jeff to run to keep up with him. Lippy trailed behind.

Jeff was scared, but tried to remain calm. They were probably going to use the rope to tie him up, but that was okay. Anything was better than . . . Jeff didn't even want to think about *that*. But when they came close to the building, Jeff changed his mind. He read the signs uneasily. DANGER. MASTER CONTROLS. HIGH-VOLTAGE SWITCHING EQUIPMENT. STAY OUT.

Even Lippy had second thoughts. "I don't like this, Fingers."

"It was your idea."

"Yeah, but I didn't know it had all this high-voltage stuff. We stick the kid in here, something could happen to him."

"So?" Fingers answered indifferently. He was examining the lock on the door. "Look at this, will you? Call this a lock?" He lifted his foot and smashed the lock with the heel of his shoe. When it broke apart, he pushed open the door and peered in. Then he motioned with his head.

"Get the kid in here. Tie him up good and put him down on the floor someplace. And let's get going. We've lost enough time. Make sure the door is closed when we leave."

"You expecting him to go someplace?" Lippy checked the tightness of the ropes he tied around Jeff's wrists and feet. "How's he going to open the door? With his teeth?" Lippy lifted Jeff and put him down in a corner of the room.

"Gag him," Fingers ordered.

"What for?" Lippy protested, noticing

how Jeff tried to pull away at the idea of something stuffed in his mouth. "Who's going to hear him?"

"Suit yourself!" Fingers snarled. He stormed out in a temper. The kid was lucky that Lippy was around, he mumbled to himself. Soft as mush when it came to kids, that's what Lippy was.

Lippy started to follow, hesitated, turned back and leaned over Jeff to whisper, "Don't start yelling, Captain. Nobody's going to hurt you, not while I'm around, okay? You only have to stay here till we dig up the money. Okay?" He reached down and gave Jeff's cap a tweak. Then, wrinkling his rabbit nose, he gave one last wave of his hand and closed the door.

Lippy rushed after his partner. It was beginning to be more trouble digging up the money than it had been robbing the bank. He never should have gotten mixed up with Fingers in the first place. Fingers was bad news.

Something else bothered Lippy as well. All the time he'd been talking to the boy, the boy's eyes had hardly blinked. He had fixed his wide, dark stare on Lippy, a steady stare without expression. Lippy couldn't tell what the boy was thinking. It wasn't natural. It made Lippy very uneasy.

However, when Lippy caught up to Fingers, who was already back at the foot of the hill, he forgot about Jeff, for the minute Fingers saw Lippy, the yellow-eyed man pointed to one of the trees and ordered, "Dig."

"Suppose this is the wrong tree?"

"Then we'll dig at the next one. And the next one after that. We'll dig under every tree until we find the money."

Lippy swallowed a sigh and picked up the shovel.

Jeff lay on the cold cement floor listening to the sound of his heart pumping away. He supposed the robbers were digging for their stolen money, but he couldn't hear a thing. At first he couldn't see anything, either. Coming in here from the outside brightness had blinded him. Now, however, his eyes were growing used to the darkness. A little light filtered in through two tiny grilles near the roof. After a while, Jeff was able to see on the wall opposite him a board on which there were rows of switches.

Jeff struggled to a sitting position. He twisted and turned his hands, trying to loosen the rope, but the knots grew tighter instead. If only he had a knife . . . He sent a searching glance around the room. There had to be some kind of tool in a place like this. But there wasn't. He sagged against the wall in frustration.

Then he had another idea. He straightened up and looked around again hopefully. What he needed was a table with sharp edges. Then he could rub his hands up and down and cut through the rope around his wrists.

There was no convenient table. He was stuck in this stupid place. He'd never get out.

Jeff was so angry — and frightened too, although he wouldn't admit it — that he flung himself down on the floor again. What was the use of even trying?

Something jabbed at his side. His eyes widened. He pushed himself up again. How dumb could he get? How could he have forgotten the boy scout knife in his pocket? He could have cheered. I'll stand on my head, he told himself. The knife will fall out. I'll work the blade free, then I'll . . .

And then he remembered that he had carefully buttoned that pocket to keep the knife from dropping out accidentally.

Disappointment stabbed at him like a sharp pain.

There was absolutely nothing he could do. There was no way he could free himself.

He glared at the wall opposite him. Switches. A lot of good they were. They reminded him a little of the switch box in the kitchen at home, the box with the fuses. He knew how to handle them. He had switched off the power, put in a new fuse, then switched the power on again the time the lamps blew in the living room.

Switches! *Power!* Jeff's eyes began to gleam. Of course! The answer was right there on the wall.

But how was Jeff, tied up like a turkey ready for the oven, going to reach up, flip a few switches and get some action going around here?

He tried wrestling again with the knots on his wrists. It was hopeless. The knots were too tight. He wriggled his feet, hoping to loosen the rope around his ankles. He could move his feet more easily than his hands, but not enough to get free.

Jeff leaned back against the wall and closed his eyes. He had to stop thinking about what he couldn't do and begin concentrating on what he might be able to do.

If I were a monkey, he told himself, I could use my tail. Picturing himself as a monkey with a long curling tail made him grin. Suddenly his eyes flew open. A monkey was like an acrobat. An acrobat could do tricks. There were some tricks Jeff could do.

Jeff's grin grew wider. He began to inch his way across the room toward the opposite wall.

•6•
Hocus Pocus
Dominocus

While Jeff was working on his plan, several other things were happening on the island.

Hugo Axel, the caretaker, had just rowed in and was coaxing his dog out of his boat, the *Islander*.

"You can do it, Gertrude," Axel crooned.

Gertrude lifted her huge head slightly and studied the caretaker through half-closed eyes. Gertrude was a Saint Bernard, and because she was enormous in size and quite old, she usually didn't much feel like moving once she was comfortable. Gertrude never stood when she could sit and never sat when she could stretch out and doze.

"I'm going to get rid of you one of these days," Axel grumbled. "See if I don't." He started to walk away without looking back.

Gertrude stared after her short, gray-haired, somewhat bowlegged master. After a while she heaved her large body up and went lumbering after Axel as he made his way toward the cottage.

Fingers and Lippy, who were now busily digging, didn't know that the caretaker and his dog had just arrived. They also didn't know that Mary Rose and Jo-Beth had reached the island some time ago.

The girls had taken the most direct route across the lake, to the swan-pedal-boat landing. All the pedal boats had been stored now that the tourist season was over. But one rowboat bobbed gently in the water.

"Look, Mary Rose. There's a rowboat tied up here. We can take that back. It'll be faster."

Mary Rose liked the idea. Pedaling was hard work after a while.

Jo-Beth was looking all around. "Hey! A signpost." She ran over to read the signs, which pointed in several directions. The signs were printed neatly on wooden boards shaped like arrows and nailed onto a thick post.

"Which way should we go?" Jo-Beth was puzzled. "Why can't we just yell good and loud?"

"I explained why. Jeff will just go and hide and we'll never find him."

"But he could be anywhere," Jo-Beth wailed. "Why don't we just go back and wait for Daddy?"

"Because we're here, that's why." Mary Rose sounded grim because she felt grim. Her sister was right. Jeff could be anywhere on the island. Judging from the number of signs, this place was a whole lot bigger than Mary Rose had thought it would be.

"Let's go to the restroom," Jo-Beth suggested promptly. "I have to go, anyway."

Mary Rose's face was a thundercloud. "You always have to go!" But then she sent her sister a thoughtful glance. "Look around while you're in there. Make sure Jeff isn't — "

"You think he's in the *ladies'* room? He'd die first, Mary Rose."

"That's exactly what Jeff would expect us to think."

Jo-Beth was shaking her head.

"Well, okay then." Mary Rose sounded exasperated. "Don't look if you don't want to. But when you come out, I want you to go see if Jeff is in the men's room."

Jo-Beth's jaw dropped. *"Me?"*

"I'm too big to go in there," Mary Rose said in her practical way. "But you're still a little kid and — "

"I am certainly *not* a little kid." Jo-Beth was insulted. "I'm seven and a half!"

"Honestly!" Mary Rose was quite cross.

Why did she have to do everything? "Never mind. I'll do it."

"You *can't,* Mary Rose. Girls can't go into a men's room."

"What's there to be afraid of? There's nobody on the island except you and me and Jeff."

Looking braver than she felt, Mary Rose knocked on the door marked MEN while Jo-Beth watched breathless, one hand pressed hard against her lips.

"Jeff? Are you in there?" Mary Rose called softly. She waited a moment, then knocked again. "Jeff?"

When there was still no answer, she inched the door open and peered in. Jeff was nowhere to be seen. The room was empty.

Turning to leave, she bumped into Jo-Beth and jumped back with a small frightened cry. "You scared me," she said furiously. "Why'd you come sneaking up behind me like that?"

"I was afraid to stay outside by myself," Jo-Beth wailed.

"I thought you were going to go to the ladies' room."

"Not by myself. You have to come with me, Mary Rose. It's kind of spooky here with nobody around at all."

"Don't you dare start imagining things, Jo-Beth Onetree." Mary Rose wouldn't admit it, but she was beginning to imagine all kinds of things too. "Come on," she added more kindly. "I'll go in with you."

As soon as they came out of the ladies' room, Mary Rose announced, "We're going to that pine grove place. It sounds like it might be a wooded area, lots of trees and bushes."

If she were going to hide, Mary Rose told herself, she would climb a tree or crouch behind a bush.

"If Jeff is up in a tree or behind a bush," Jo-Beth said, reading her sister's mind again, "how will we ever find him?"

"We might be able to hear him moving around."

Jo-Beth thought it was a dumb idea, but she knew she couldn't talk her sister out of doing what she had decided to do. Mary

Rose was so used to making decisions that she never asked Jo-Beth what she thought.

They really ought to go back and get their father. He'd know what to do. But Mary Rose was so bossy. She never listened to Jo-Beth. They'd probably go on looking for Jeff until they were old ladies with take-out teeth, like Mrs. MacGruder, who lived down the street from their house.

Her thoughts kept Jo-Beth busy until the girls reached the hill and peered down. No one was in sight, because Fingers and Lippy were just putting Jeff into the switch-control building. By the time the men returned to start their digging, the girls had left the grove and were on their way to the amusement park.

"I'm getting awfully tired," Jo-Beth complained. "I want to go home."

Mary Rose was rather tired too, but she had made up her mind that they wouldn't leave the island until they found Jeff.

When the girls reached the amusement area and the rides, Jo-Beth spied a small train with seats for two in rows one behind the other.

"I'm sitting down," Jo-Beth said emphatically. She ran to the little train station, jumped into the train and sat down with a great sigh of relief. Mary Rose hesitated, then went to sit beside her sister.

"Only for a minute," she announced firmly.

Jo-Beth smiled. "Look," she pointed. "A merry-go-round. It must be nice here in the summertime when it's busy and the music is playing and the kids are running around. And you can smell the hot dogs and the popcorn and the french fries . . . I'm getting awfully hungry, Mary Rose."

"You're always hungry. Come on. Let's go."

But Jo-Beth was leaning back with a dreamy air. If she had a magic wand, Jo-Beth thought, she would wave it around, and hocus pocus dominocus, everything would start up and . . .

It was exactly at that moment that the merry-go-round began to turn. Loud music tore the quietness apart. Some of the horses started to move up and down. The train in which they were sitting gave a hard jerk, knocking them forward and then backward, and then rattled along the tracks toward a long, low building sitting directly in their path.

Jo-Beth just had a moment to read a sign — TUNNEL OF TERROR — before two doors swung open and the girls were plunged into darkness.

•7•
The Tunnel of Terror

Jo-Beth huddled against her sister.

"I can't see!" she cried. "The dark is blinding me!"

Mary Rose knew how her sister felt about the dark. Even at home with the whole family there, Jo-Beth liked to have a small lamp on all night.

"It's just a silly ride," Mary Rose explained; just the same, she held tight to her sister's hand.

"Then why do they call it the Tunnel of Terror? That doesn't sound like just a ride."

"Oh, I guess they'll have the usual witches and black cats and skeletons, like they do at the Halloween House back home . . . "

"Are you sure, Mary Rose?"

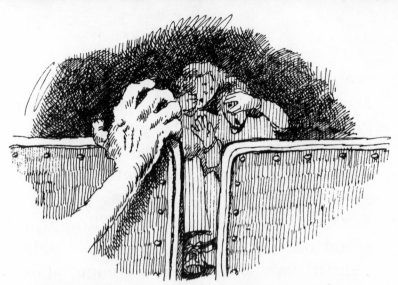

"Sure I'm sure. These things are always the same. What else could it be?"

Jo-Beth tried to reply, but all she could do was make a small strangled sound. She was staring at the front of the car. Long, green, glowing, bony fingers were slowly, very slowly, inching over the rim of the car in which they sat.

Mary Rose gasped and for a moment seemed too paralyzed to move. Then suddenly she ripped a sneaker from her foot and whacked at the creeping fingers as hard as she could. The fingers jerked up, trembled in the air and fell back.

The older girl sighed with relief, but her sister turned around and peered fearfully at the back of the train.

Suppose the fingers were there? Would they keep coming? Would they reach out and grab the girls in a terrible grip and . . .

"I think I'm going to faint," Jo-Beth said, and started to weave back and forth in her seat.

"Don't you dare faint," Mary Rose whispered back in a furious voice. She didn't want to face whatever was coming alone. "It's your fault we're here. It was your dumb idea to sit down in this dumb train."

While she was talking, the color of the walls changed from blood red to a constantly shimmering dismal gray. The shimmering made the girls feel that the walls were moving in one direction as they moved in another. Curling mists of fog rose and swirled in the air.

"Why are the walls moving?" Jo-Beth complained immediately. "Walls aren't supposed to move. They're supposed to stand still."

Before her sister could answer, they heard the pounding of a horse's hooves echoing through the tunnel. They were afraid to look back and afraid not to. It *was* a horse, with a man crouching on its back.

A cold wind began to blow, chilling the girls. It moaned and shrieked and made a sobbing sound as it whistled past them.

The rider's cloak billowed out behind him. Horse and rider were led by an eerie lengthening shadow that was catching up to them rapidly.

"Mary Rose!" Jo-Beth tried to swallow but couldn't. *"He doesn't have a head!"*

"Yes, he does," Mary Rose replied shakily. "He's carrying it. Under his arm. Don't look, Jo-Beth! Don't look!" she shouted as the rider began to pass.

But it was too late.

The rider had turned and thrust his head straight at them. The dead eyes fixed them with a hideous glare; the lips parted in a terrible grin.

Jo-Beth buried her face in her hands. "I'm not going to look at another thing in here. Just tell me when it's all over. Unless I die first," she couldn't help adding. She slumped against her sister and let her head sag.

Mary Rose was going to push her up, but

decided instead to put her arm around her sister. They ought not to allow children on a ride like this, she thought angrily. For the moment she had quite forgotten that there had been no one around to stop them.

"Just keep your eyes closed till I tell you to open them," she comforted her sister. She didn't want to look either, but she couldn't seem to turn her gaze away. So she saw the giant spider that zoomed down from the ceiling, and the snakes hanging from the twisted branches of peculiar trees, and the threatening eyes without faces that dangled and twisted in midair like a hideous mobile.

Jo-Beth, meanwhile, had clamped her hands over her ears to shut out the queer noises that boomed at them from everywhere in the tunnel — crazy laughter, drawn-out wails and pitiful whimpers.

And then all the noise stopped.

Jo-Beth opened one eye cautiously, in time to see directly ahead, blocking the tracks, a gigantic purple woolly monster. Its nose was a wide, ugly snout, with one wicked-looking bone pointing straight up just above the snout. Its eyes were fierce behind a dark mask. And its mouth was as huge as the opening to a cave.

"Mary Rose." Jo-Beth's words came out in a shriek. "I want to get off this train."

Mary Rose pulled her sister close. "He's not real. He's not real."

"I'm the purple people eater!" the monster roared.

Jo-Beth huddled back in her seat. "But we're not purple. Tell him we're not purple, Mary Rose."

The monster's mouth opened wider. Before Mary Rose could say a word, the train picked up speed, heading directly for the waiting mouth.

"Just tell me when we're dead!" Jo-Beth gasped.

Swooooosh! The train raced into the mouth, and the girls were swallowed by darkness. They clutched each other, too frightened even to scream. Mary Rose was first to notice a dim red light in the monster's throat.

"It's all right. It's all right. Look, Jo-Beth. See that red light? It's an exit."

Even as she spoke, two doors flew open, and the train zoomed out the exit into the welcome sunshine.

Jo-Beth ran her fingers over her arms and body as if to make sure she was still in one piece. "Are we still alive?" she asked with surprise.

Now that they were out in the open, Mary Rose felt quite brave. "Of course we are. I told you it was just a ride. All that icky stuff in there. I don't know why we got so scared. We knew all the time it wasn't real, not any of it."

"I'm getting off this crazy train," Jo-Beth announced positively.

Mary Rose was still busy with her own thoughts. "I don't know why amusement parks have these scary rides."

"Why do they call it 'amusement'?" Jo-Beth was indignant. "It's no fun to be scared to death. If I'm going to be scared, I like to know about it ahead of time. I don't like it here." She gave her sister an accusing look. "You told me the island was closed. How come this train started to go, anyway?"

She realized as she spoke that the train was still rushing along.

"I want to get off."

"You just said that a minute ago."

"I don't care how many times I said it. *I want to get off,*" Jo-Beth said, spacing out her words for emphasis.

"Okay. Just tell me one thing: How do we get the train to stop?"

Jo-Beth stared at her sister. A cold feeling trickled down her spine. Of course! Someone had bewitched them! They would have to stay on this train riding round and round forever. Doomed to go through the Tunnel of Terror over and over again.

She shuddered. Nothing worse could possibly happen.

Just then Mary Rose moaned, "Oh, no!"

Jo-Beth was afraid to ask, but she had to know. "What is it? What's the matter now?"

•8•
Land of the
Dreadful Dragons

"Look." Mary Rose pointed to a sign just ahead.

"'Land of the Dreadful Dragons,'" Jo-Beth read. "Mary Rose, please. Do something."

"Like what? You want me to wave my hands around, yell 'Abracadabra' and make the train stop?"

"I don't like dragons," Jo-Beth said tearfully. "I've always hated dragons."

"You've never even ever seen a dragon," Mary Rose began, then stopped when she saw her sister's woebegone expression. She put an arm around the younger girl. "I can't stop the train, Jo-Beth. I wish I could. Just try to remember this is only a ride too."

The train had already approached the

entrance. Two fierce dragons, with forked tongues flickering through dagger-sharp fangs, stood on tiptoe and reached across space to seize each other with their scaly arms, forming an arch. The train plunged through this arch and into the Land of the Dreadful Dragons.

There were dragons everywhere, big ones and little ones, sitting or leaping or fighting. All were a poisonous green color, with shiny scales and long, slashing tails. Some had horns. Some had webbed, batlike wings. Their bulging eyes flashed red lightning. They groaned and hissed and roared, making sounds like thunder rolling in from a great distance. They turned toward the train as it passed by, snatching at it with their long, sharp claws. One dragon seemed to miss the girls by inches.

"Watch out!" Mary Rose cried. They moved closer to one another and clutched hands.

The train had been climbing slowly but steadily. Jo-Beth had to clap one hand over her mouth. This new ride was turning into a roller coaster. She hated roller coasters.

Her stomach began to jump. Her stomach jumped even when she had to ride in an elevator.

"Don't look down," Mary Rose commanded. It was only a small roller coaster, but Mary Rose knew any height made Jo-Beth dizzy.

Jo-Beth leaned back in her seat and looked up instead of down, directly into the mean, raging eyes of another dragon. His tongue streaked toward her. A voice rasped through the gaping jaws: "Here's a tasty dish for a hungry dragon."

"Mary Rose!"

Before Mary Rose could respond, the train dipped down. Jo-Beth clamped her eyes shut as hard as she could. Maybe she would be lucky and die before they hit bottom. Mary Rose would be sorry then, all

right. She would be sorry she had taken her poor little sister away from a nice safe house to an island where people carried their heads under their arms and dreadful dragons talked.

The train was near the ground again, chugging along at a good pace.

Mary Rose suddenly began to giggle. "Look, Jo-Beth. Come on. You can look. This is funny."

Jo-Beth stole a peek through narrowed eyes. A large dragon, dressed in an orange uniform with rows of sparkling gold buttons and a cap marked *Dragon School,* was sitting at a desk. Behind the desk was a blackboard on which was written: WHAT EVERY DRAGON MUST KNOW: LESSON ONE. BREATHING FIRE. A number of quite small dragons were sitting in a circle around the desk. As the train rushed by, the giant dragon moved a pointer to the word *fire.* At the same time, the tiny dragons turned their heads and blew smoke from their nostrils.

Jo-Beth smiled, but it was a small smile. "Can't we get off?" she asked faintly.

Mary Rose had been wondering the same

thing. But how? She supposed they could work their way over the seats to the end of the train, jump off when the train slowed down and walk back along the tracks. But that would mean going through the Tunnel of Terror. They couldn't stand that again. Well, maybe there was an emergency brake on the front of the train. But when she peered over the rim of their seat, she could see no handle or button or wheel that she could yank or press or turn. Then she began to study the roller coaster as it rose and dipped. At some places the tracks seemed to run fairly close to the ground.

She grabbed her sister's arm. "Listen. We're coming up to a really low place just up ahead. When I say 'Jump,' you jump. Right away. Understand, Jo-Beth?"

Jo-Beth pulled away, shaking her head. "I can't jump out of anything that's moving."

"I'll hold you. Jump, Jo-Beth. Jump."

But Jo-Beth simply shrank back into her seat as far as she could and stared at her sister with wide, frightened eyes.

"I'm so mad I could spit," Mary Rose shouted at her, for now the train had picked up speed and was climbing again. And straight ahead, at the top of the curve, a dragon was beginning to rest its huge head directly on the tracks.

"We're going to crash right into him. Oh, please," Jo-Beth said prayerfully. "Somebody please save us from the dreadful dragons."

The train rattled on, closer and closer. At the very last moment, seconds away from a collision, the dragon lifted its head skyward. Its scaly arms rested inches away from the train. And the dragon froze in that position. There was a screeching of wheels, and the train came to a dead stop.

For a moment the girls just sat there, paralyzed, afraid that the train would begin moving again or that the dragon would drop its fearsome head. Then Mary Rose whispered, as if someone might be listening, "Now's our chance, Jo-Beth."

Her sister glanced down. "Chance?" she asked. "Chance for what? How are we going to get way down there?" She waved her hand at the ground.

Mary Rose started pulling at her lower lip with her thumb and forefinger.

"You have an idea." Jo-Beth knew her sister would think of something. She could depend on Mary Rose.

"We're going to climb down the dragon."

"Not me," Jo-Beth said promptly. "I'm not climbing down any old dragon. Not me."

"Are you expecting somebody to come and get us?" Mary Rose asked reasonably. "Or do you just want to stay here and wait?"

The way Mary Rose said that, it sounded as if they might have to wait forever. Jo-Beth looked down again and then back at the dragon. "You can't just climb down . . . I mean, how would we do it?"

"It won't be that hard, Jo-Beth. Honestly! You see how the scales on the dragon are made? They're like little steps. Just try to make believe you're climbing down a ladder."

Mary Rose stood up carefully and stepped out onto the narrow path beside the tracks. Then, very cautiously, she reached out and clutched one of the scales.

"See?" she called back with an air of confidence. "Just follow me and do what I do. If we go real slow, just take our time and don't look down, it won't be too bad."

Jo-Beth took a deep breath. Some ladder, she thought, as she, too, grasped a scale.

Jo-Beth was always very good at imagining all sorts of impossible things, but not once had she ever dreamed that she would find herself on a deserted island climbing down the back of a raging dragon!

•9•
Digging a Hole
to China

When they were safely on the ground again, the girls glanced at the many dragons, all of them motionless in different positions, some leaning, some hesitating in midstep, some caught in terrible battle.

As she and Mary Rose walked quickly toward the exit along a path that passed the dragon arch, Jo-Beth said, "I wonder who stopped the dragons."

"It's who *started* them that I'm wondering about." Mary Rose had been doing some hard thinking on the climb down and the walk back through the Land of the Dreadful Dragons. "I'll bet Jeff found out we were looking for him and tried to scare us off the island."

"That's the meanest thing I ever heard

of." Jo-Beth's face flushed with anger. "If you ask me, I think we should stop looking for him right now. I think it would serve him right if we got in the boat and went back this minute."

"And tell Daddy we gave up looking for Jeff just because he made us mad?"

Jo-Beth sighed. She supposed they would have to keep searching. But if Jeff was acting this way now, what would it be like when he came to live with them?

"What I don't understand," Mary Rose went on, busy with her own thoughts, "is if the island is closed and everything is all locked up, how did Jeff start the rides?"

That was what Lippy and Fingers were wondering as well.

Fingers had chosen one of the two trees under which, he was positive, the money was hidden. The two men had begun to dig quickly. Lippy had been staring down into the hole and muttering, "The way this looks, if we go any deeper we'll wind up in China," when the merry-go-round suddenly blared out its canned music. Lippy had

been so startled that he had slipped and fallen into the hole. Fingers had leaped backward, tripped over a large root extending from the tree and landed on his skull. For a moment his head spun.

"What was that?" Lippy exclaimed, climbing up out of the hole and brushing off the loose dirt. "I must be going crazy. It sounded just like a merry-go-round."

Fingers was rubbing his head. Both men could now also hear a train making clickety sounds along a track.

"I thought you said this place was closed.

You said it was better than a deserted island. You said — "

"Will you shut up?" Fingers demanded. "Don't tell me what I said. It's that kid. He must have got the rides started somehow." He started to run toward the small brick building in which they had imprisoned Jeff.

Lippy pounded after his partner. "But how did he do it? He was tied up good. When I tie somebody up, he stays tied up. So how did he do it?"

That was the question that Fingers asked, with a hard, mean look, when they opened the door and found Jeff still inside and still very much bound hand and foot.

"Okay," Fingers said after he turned off the switches. "How'd you do it?"

Jeff was sitting just where the men had left him. He asked innocently, "How'd I do what?"

"Turn the switches on, you smart-aleck kid. When I ask you a question, I want an answer," Fingers said roughly.

Jeff thought quickly. He remembered a movie he had seen where a boy had thought hard, very hard, and then stared, his eyes strange and fixed, and made awful things happen. He started fires and made objects fly through the air . . . "I concentrated," Jeff said. "I have the power!"

"I knew it," Lippy said, sounding uneasy. "I had a feeling . . . I mean, that look in his eyes, it isn't natural. No offense, Captain," he added hastily.

Jeff tried not to grin. Lippy *believed* him!

"Can you try not being so stupid?" Fingers roared at Lippy. Then he stepped closer to Jeff, clenching his hand into a fist.

"Listen, kid. Cut out the funny stuff. Nobody makes a fool of me, understand?"

He brought his fist up.

Lippy stepped quickly between the two. Maybe Fingers was right. Maybe Lippy was being stupid. But wasn't there such a thing as the evil eye? Why take chances?

Jeff, meanwhile, was preparing himself to be brave. Even if Fingers hit him, he wouldn't tell him anything.

"I ought to put you out like a light." Fingers stepped even closer.

Lippy was alarmed. "Wait a minute, Fingers. I told you no rough stuff. Even if the captain here turned on a couple of kid rides somehow. So what?"

"Suppose they heard the noise over on the mainland?"

"So they heard it. So they think somebody · turned on a radio. Who pays attention to loud music?"

Fingers continued to glare at Jeff. Reluctantly he said at last, "Yeah."

Jeff tried to keep from looking triumphant. *He* knew someone who would pay attention. Hugo Axel and his wife had a house right on the edge of the lake, directly across from the island. The caretaker would recognize the sound of the merry-go-round. He'd be rushing over to investigate.

Fingers made sure everything that could be turned off in the little building was definitely off. Then he said to Lippy, "Bring the kid," and went out the door.

Lippy lifted Jeff to his feet and slung him over his shoulder. "What're we going to do with him?"

"We're going to tie him to a tree."

"Which tree?"

"What do I care which tree?" Fingers was

78

exasperated. "Any tree. Someplace away from here where I don't have to look at him. And stick a gag in his mouth."

"You don't have to gag me," Jeff called from over Lippy's shoulder. "I won't yell or anything."

"I know you won't," Fingers said ominously. Struck by a sudden thought, he added, "Wait a minute, Lippy, before you gag him. Kid, what did you do with your boat? Where'd you park it?"

"You don't *park* a boat," Jeff began, and stopped when he saw the icy glitter in the slit yellow tiger eyes. "It's . . . uh . . . it's at the ferry landing."

Fingers reached over, knocked off Jeff's cap and grabbed him by the hair, forcing Jeff's head up and back. He continued to hold on as he spoke: "You're a smart kid, right? So if I go there and don't find it, what's going to happen to you when I come back all riled up? Tell him what I'm like when I'm riled up, Lippy."

Lippy shook his head. He didn't even want to think about it. "Don't be a hero, Captain. Just tell him where the boat is."

Jeff swallowed hard. Fingers' knuckles were grinding into his skull. He knew it would get much worse if he didn't tell Fingers what he wanted to know.

"It's over near the caretaker's shed. You're not going to take it, are you?" Jeff asked anxiously.

"I'm not going to take it — "

Jeff sighed with relief.

" — I'm going to sink it. Gag him and let's go, Lippy." The man with the tiger eyes strode off.

Lippy picked up Jeff's cap, brushed it off and put it back on Jeff's head. Then he pulled a large crumpled handkerchief from his pocket. "Sorry, Captain. That's the breaks."

"You think it's fair to push a kid around?" Jeff asked.

Lippy was surprised. "You got a lot to learn. Everybody gets pushed around."

"Grown-ups don't."

Lippy laughed. "You think not?" He shook his head. "You sure do have a lot to learn. Now open your mouth. I won't make the gag too tight," he whispered.

Lippy tied Jeff securely to a tree, well out of sight of the equipment building. Then he started to move away, hesitated, came back and said somewhat sheepishly, "Uh, listen, Captain. We don't mean you no harm. Honest. All we want is to get our money and go. So could you please not . . . " He stopped talking and tapped his forefinger against his left eye. "You know what I mean. Fingers is getting real mad."

He tested the knots once more and then hurried off after his partner. Fingers had made it all sound so simple. All they had to do was row out to this island, find the two rocks, measure the ropes to a point, dig and — bingo! — they'd have the money. Then it would be South America, Argentina maybe, and the rich life.

Lippy should have been warned when they couldn't find the rocks. When a job starts to turn sour, the best thing is to forget it. But Fingers wasn't Lippy. Fingers never gave up on anything, no matter what.

It was the no-matter-what that was worrying Lippy right now.

•10•
What Happened
to the Hole?

Jeff didn't like being tied to a tree. He didn't like having a dirty handkerchief stuffed in his mouth, either. The thing to do, he told himself, is to take deep breaths through the nose and try to concentrate on other things.

He turned his mind toward all the sound that had exploded when he threw the switches. Old Hugo must have had a fit when he heard the merry-go-round. He must have shot out of his house like a rocket. He was probably halfway to the island already.

Jeff was right about one thing. Old Hugo did have a fit. He was in the caretaker's cottage when he heard all the noise. He couldn't believe it. Somebody had turned on the rides. Whatever for?

Hugo pressed his lips together in a hard, tight line. He didn't doubt for a minute that some kids were fooling around on the island. Well, Hugo would put a stop to that in a hurry. No vandals were going to start trouble on Hugo Axel's island. No, sir!

He left the cottage in such a hurry that he neglected to coax Gertrude to come along. This was so unusual that Gertrude got up and trotted after him out of curiosity.

Just as Hugo reached the pine grove, two things happened: All the sound stopped. It was so quiet again that the caretaker could hear Gertrude's heavy breathing. Hugo shook his head with pity. The poor old creature couldn't even take a quick walk anymore without panting.

The second thing that happened was that Hugo suddenly caught sight of the deep hole the two bank robbers had dug. The caretaker's face stained crimson red as he looked at it.

What in the world would make anybody

come to this peaceful place and start tearing it up?

He knew right away that kids were responsible. The island was private and restful and beautiful most of the year, until the tourists came with their kids. Then, Hugo always told himself, it was like living with a buzzsaw that never shut off.

With the rides silent, Hugo forgot for a moment that he had been heading for the equipment building. All he could think of was this big hole next to the pine tree. Noticing the spade Lippy had left behind, Hugo seized it and began to shovel the dirt back into the hole. He worked hard and fast, muttering all the time.

Gertrude dozed, stretched out full length under the tree beside the one where the hole had been dug. Hugo stood up, straightened his back and put the spade against the tree. The hole was filled in, but the ground around it wasn't tidy enough to suit him. The caretaker spread earth over the area evenly with his hands, sprinkled leaves over the dirt and finally flicked a few branches over the whole area. At last he was satisfied. No one would ever know that a hole had been dug in this spot.

"Come on, Gertrude. We better go see who was fooling around with the switches."

Gertrude barely opened her eyes. She had no intention of moving. She watched the caretaker walk off and settled her huge head more comfortably between her paws.

When Hugo reached the equipment building, he stopped and glared at the broken lock. He pulled it from the hinge and shook it in the air. "Will you look at that?" he raged. "Will you just look at that?"

He flung open the door and shouted, "Listen, whoever you are . . . " But no one was there. Hugo checked all the switches. Everything was exactly as it should be, except for the lock. He would search for the kids later. Right now he had to go back to the cottage and find another lock. Forgetting about Gertrude, Hugo walked on slowly, staring at the broken lock every once in a while and muttering to himself all over again.

He just missed Lippy and Fingers, who had found Hugo's boat, the *Islander*, and sunk it. They had taken for granted that it was Jeff's boat, since it was the only one they saw.

Lippy wasn't happy. "Why'd we have to sink the kid's boat? How's he going to get back?"

"That's the whole idea, stupid. Now there's no way he can leave and go to the cops."

"But he's tied up."

"He was tied up when he turned on those switches somehow, wasn't he? We'll see how smart the kid is when we take off and he's still tied to that tree."

Lippy didn't like any of this at all. Suppose a wild animal came along? That's what he asked Fingers. The other man's laugh sent shivers up Lippy's spine. Fingers would like that, Lippy realized. Fingers would like that just fine.

But Fingers shook his head. "A wild animal in this place? Listen, you clunk, you probably think a squirrel is a wild animal."

"Never mind what I think!" Lippy's sudden anger took Fingers by surprise. "We're not leaving that kid on this island tied up."

"Who says we're not?" Fingers asked, his voice dangerous.

"You want me to help find the money?"

"Okay. Keep your shirt on. You can call the sheriff when we get back to the town and tell him where the kid is if you want to."

Lippy nodded.

"If the kid doesn't use his power and blow up the island first," Fingers jeered.

"You shouldn't joke about that. A lot of weird things happen that nobody can explain. They happen all the time — " Lippy stopped in midsentence. The two men had reached the hill while they were talking. Now Lippy suddenly spotted Gertrude. "There's a horse under that tree! Where'd it come from?"

"That's not a horse. It's a dog." Fingers' mind was occupied with something more important. "The hole!" he raged. "What happened to the hole?"

Lippy's gaze took in the smoothed-over ground. He shivered. He couldn't help it.

That little kid had been telling the truth

after all. He did have the power. No. It wasn't possible.

Was it?

No.

Still, *where was the hole?*

•11•
The Big Orange Bird

The loud voices of the two men woke Gertrude. She lifted her head slightly, her old brain reminding her that a dog had certain duties. When she remembered that one of them was to protect property, she let out a small growl. Of course, because of Gertrude's size, even a small growl sounded threatening.

Lippy stepped back hastily, but Fingers stayed where he was.

"This must be the kid's dog." He smacked his fist into the palm of his other hand. "That kid has been nothing but trouble since we laid eyes on him. Go see if he's still tied up."

While Lippy was gone, Fingers stood and stared with disbelief at the ground where the hole had once been. They had been away only a short time. How could the kid have gotten loose and shoveled the dirt back in so fast? He knew Lippy was beginning to believe that the kid could do some hocus pocus with his eyes and his thoughts, but Fingers knew better. Somebody must have untied the kid. Then they'd come back here . . .

Lippy came racing back to report that the boy was exactly where they had left him. He did not report that he had apologized as he checked the ropes. "I'm real sorry about your boat, Captain. We had to knock a couple of holes in it, but maybe you can get somebody to fix it up for you. Nice name you had on it, too. *Islander.*" He had tweaked Jeff's cap again, but hadn't noticed Jeff's look of surprise and joy.

Lippy had started to leave, then came back. "Uh . . . listen, Captain. You didn't . . . *do* anything while we were gone, did you?"

Jeff tried to say something through the gag in his mouth.

"Never mind. You couldn't . . . never

mind." He left quickly. Things he couldn't understand made him nervous.

"Maybe the kid was telling the truth," Lippy was now saying, as much to himself as to his partner. "He couldn't have done it. Maybe he did come to the island with a whole bunch of boy scouts." Lippy stared at the ground sadly. "There goes the ball game, right?"

"Wrong. I'm not letting a bunch of kids scare me away. We're not leaving without the money, and that's final." Fingers had it all figured out. As Lippy had said, they had dug a hole practically to China and found nothing. The money must be under the tree beside it, the tree that the dog had claimed.

Fingers moved a little closer, very cautiously. "Nice doggie," he said in a too-sugary voice. "Good boy." He picked up a branch and hurled it through the air. "There you go. Go get the stick. Come on, boy. Go get it."

Gertrude gazed at Fingers. She had no idea what he was talking about. While she tried to figure it out, she fell asleep.

"Miserable dog," Fingers snapped. "We'll just have to move him."

"*Move* him?" Lippy looked at Gertrude as if he were gazing up the side of a small mountain. He couldn't believe it. "How?"

"How do you think?" Fingers was growing more short-tempered by the minute. "We lift him, that's how."

"*Lift* him?"

"Listen, stupid. You repeat one more thing I say and I'll hammer you into the ground with my bare fists." To make sure his partner knew what he meant, Fingers waved one of those fists under Lippy's nose.

"Okay. Okay. Anything you say," Lippy told him hastily. He edged closer to Gertrude, who was now snoring. "Good dog," Lippy said, reaching down to pat her gingerly.

"You grab the back legs and I'll take the front. When I count to three, just heave him up," Fingers said. "Ready? Okay. One. Two. THREE."

The veins stood out on Fingers' knobby forehead. Lippy's eyes began to pop. Gertrude didn't budge an inch.

"You know what?" Lippy gasped when he

could catch his breath. "I think we'd be better off pulling him."

The two men stationed themselves on each side of the dog and tugged. Once in a while they went behind Gertrude and pushed.

"We'd be better off on a rock pile, making little rocks out of big ones," Lippy complained, breathing heavily.

Suddenly Gertrude awoke. She didn't like being tugged at from all sides. She growled deep in her throat, a growl that made the men drop her quickly. Gertrude ruffled her fur and then slowly got up and walked away. Fingers threw a stick at her in anger, but since it missed her, Gertrude continued along the path.

"All right. Now he's off the spot, let's get at the digging," Fingers said. "The sooner we get out of here, the better I'll like it."

The two men dug quickly and silently. Lippy promised himself that as soon as they got off the island, he would make that call to the sheriff. He wouldn't give his name, naturally. He'd just say he was a well-wisher. That was good. He liked that. A well-wisher. That way he wouldn't have the kid on his conscience.

Lippy wasn't the only one who was thinking about Jeff. Mary Rose and Jo-Beth had left the Land of the Dreadful Dragons and had searched the playground and picnic area.

"Are you sure Jeff came to the island?" Jo-Beth asked at last.

It was depressing walking around, just the two of them, with not another living soul anywhere. The swings were motionless; the seesaws rested at a tilt; the slides waited for children who were not there. The picnic tables and benches had a waiting look too.

It was as if the two of them were the only ones left on earth! What if that was true?

What if Jeff and everyone in the whole world had vanished?

Jo-Beth could picture herself and Mary Rose taking their pedal boat back to the mainland and finding people and animals mysteriously gone, shutters flapping in the wind, papers whirling through the streets of the town. Jo-Beth could feel tears begin to sting her eyes. She and Mary Rose would never know what had happened. They would wander from village to village . . .

"I guess we might as well go back to the boat," Mary Rose said, breaking into Jo-Beth's fantasy. "Maybe you're right. We'll never find Jeff here. There are too many places to look."

Jo-Beth stole a look at her sister's unhappy face. "It wasn't your fault," she said loyally. "You did everything you could."

She glanced around. Now that they were ready to leave, Jo-Beth felt better about the island. It wasn't a bad place, with the birds singing and the leaves crunching underfoot. Once in a while she even caught sight of the birds as they flitted from one place to another. Some of the birds seemed to prefer the low-hanging branches of trees. Others vanished into bushes and then popped out again. Birds were such restless creatures, always in motion. But she could see one bird — she guessed it was a bird — that wasn't moving at all. She wondered if the bird was so still because it had hurt its wing or had gotten stuck in the bush. It *was* kind of large. And so, orange.

"What do you call those big orange birds?" Jo-Beth asked.

"How should I know?" Mary Rose answered impatiently. Then she studied her sister. "Are you pretending again, or did you see something?"

Jo-Beth pointed. "Is that pretend?"

Mary Rose put her fingers to her lips. She began to tiptoe toward the bush. As the girls came closer, they could hear choking sounds.

"What is it?" Jo-Beth whispered. She got behind her sister just in case the big orange bird turned out to be a monster. After the events of this day, that wouldn't surprise her. Anything could happen on this island, anything at all.

•12•
The Great Pedal-Boat Escape

"It's Jeff!" Mary Rose gasped, bounding out of her hiding place.

"Who tied you up?" Jo-Beth cried, close on her sister's heels.

Jeff was still making the odd sounds they had heard, trying desperately to talk through the gag in his mouth. As soon as Mary Rose untied the handkerchief, Jeff said accusingly, "You followed me. I told you in my letter I could take care of myself, didn't I?"

"We can see what a great job you're doing taking care of yourself," Mary Rose said angrily. "Why'd you have to run away? Do you know what we've been through, trying to find you?"

"Who tied you up?" Jo-Beth was in a

frenzy. What was the matter with them, starting an argument now? She tried to loosen the knots in the rope, but they were too tight.

"My father is going to be awfully mad at you," Mary Rose went on. "And he'll be mad at me, and it isn't even my fault."

"Grown-ups are always mad about something. What are you doing?" he asked Jo-Beth irritably.

"I'm looking for your boy scout knife in one of your pockets. Maybe you and Mary Rose want to stand here all day and yell at each other, but I want to go home."

Mary Rose was surprised. While she had lost her temper, daydreaming, play-acting, Jo-Beth was sensibly searching for a knife to cut the ropes.

"Look in my back pocket, the one that's buttoned. I tried to unbutton it, but I couldn't with my hands tied like this."

Jo-Beth found the knife but was afraid to open it. Mary Rose dug her fingernail gingerly into the groove of the handle, flicking the blade out carefully.

"Don't move," she warned as she began to saw away at the ropes.

"What happened, Jeff? Who tied you up?" Jo-Beth repeated.

As Jeff explained, Jo-Beth grew more and more excited. Why, this was more thrilling than anything she could dream up, and it was all true!

"I knew it was you." Mary Rose smiled knowingly when Jeff came to the part where he had been locked up. Before he could explain how he had turned on the switches, Jo-Beth broke in eagerly, "But you were tied up. How could you start the rides all tied up?"

Jeff gave his cousin a solemn stare. "Look into my eyes," he commanded, dropping his voice so that it was low and deep. "Do you see the pupils?"

"No," Jo-Beth whispered. "I don't."

"That's because I'm different," he went on, still speaking in that strange tone of voice. "I can do anything. I have the power!"

"Oh, stop it," Mary Rose scolded. "You're scaring her. What really happened? And why did you do it? You gave us a terrible time." She grew angry just remembering the Tunnel of Terror and the Land of the Dreadful Dragons. And she grew even angrier at Jeff for laughing when Jo-Beth broke in to describe their adventures in both places.

"Well, how was I to know?" Jeff said. "Anyway, what else could I do? I couldn't get free."

"What did you *do*?" Jo-Beth wanted Jeff to get on with his explanation.

"I wriggled across the floor. It felt like it took me forever. When I got to the board on the other side of the room, I balanced myself on my head by wriggling my feet up against the wall and sort of leaning on my elbows. And then I just kicked on the switches that I could reach."

"What good did you think that was going to do?" Mary Rose wondered. "Didn't you know it would only make those guys mad?"

"I had to do it. I wanted to get old Hugo's attention. He's the caretaker. And I sure did, because he's on the island right now."

"How do you know?"

"Because they sank his boat. They sank the *Islander*." Jeff rubbed his hands and then his ankles as the ropes fell away. He started to remove his vest. "Those guys would never have seen me if it hadn't been for this vest."

"Neither would we," Mary Rose reminded him. "You know where we can find old Hugo? We better go and — "

"No," Jeff said at once. "The first thing we have to do is prevent those guys from getting off the island with the money. We've got to find their boat and disable it."

"I know where it is," Jo-Beth said eagerly. "We saw a rowboat at the pedal-boat place, remember, Mary Rose?"

"Follow me. And don't make a sound," Jeff warned. They tiptoed Indian style, one behind the other, with Jeff leading the way.

"See?" Jo-Beth said when they reached the pedal-boat landing. She pointed to a boat bobbing in the water.

Jeff whistled. "That's no little rowboat. That's one of the dories Hugo rents out to fishermen." He studied the dory with its high flaring sides and sharp bow. "That's going to be hard to scuttle."

"What's 'scuttle'?" Jo-Beth asked. "It sounds horrible."

"That's sea talk. It means we're going to have to sink it. We have to make some holes in the boat so it can't be used." He looked around. "Try to find some heavy rocks with sharp edges."

The three children scouted the beach. The girls brought their rocks to Jeff for inspection. When he was satisfied, they went back to the water's edge.

"Let's get the boat on the beach," Jeff ordered.

"Our clothes will get soaked," Jo-Beth protested.

"Don't be such a little kid," Jeff said, sounding annoyed.

"Well, I am a little kid." Jo-Beth stopped talking because Mary Rose and Jeff were already wading out to the boat.

"You girls pull and I'll push." Jeff got behind the dory. It moved easily toward the beach while it was still in the water. But they couldn't drag it up on the sand, no matter how hard they pushed.

"This old dory is too heavy," Jeff admitted at last. "We've got it up a little way. Now let's get in and start working on the bottom."

Kneeling in the boat, they began to hammer away. Jo-Beth's hands turned an angry red after a while; Mary Rose's arms began to ache.

"I'm tired," Jo-Beth complained.

"Me too," Mary Rose admitted.

Jeff paid no attention. Instead, he began to twist his rock round and round. After a while, he raised his head and grinned at his cousins. "Anybody want to see a nice big hole in this boat?"

The girls grinned back with delight.

"Let's push the dory as far out as we can," Jeff said.

It seemed like less work, getting the dory into the water. They felt like cheering when they saw it begin to sink.

"I can still see it, though, right through the water." Jo-Beth was worried.

She was right. The boat was plainly visible in the clear, quiet water.

"That's all right," Jeff told her. "Nobody's going anywhere in this boat, believe me. Now," he went on in a businesslike way, "we've got to get the pedal boat hidden."

"We ought to get help," Mary Rose interrupted.

Jeff clapped his hand over her mouth. "*Sssh,*" he hissed. "They're coming. I hear them. Quick. Hide. Don't let them see us."

The three fled along the bank and scurried behind a large bush. Jo-Beth was certain the men would hear her heart thumping wildly.

Lippy was first to spot that he and his partner were in big trouble.

"The boat's gone. Somebody stole our boat!"

"It's not gone, lunkhead. Somebody sank it." Fingers stared at the dory with fury.

"Who'd do a rotten thing like that?" Lippy asked. But he knew the answer. The kid had really fixed them this time. He was a jinx. Ever since they first laid eyes on him, he had caused them nothing but trouble.

Lippy didn't doubt for a moment that the kid had sunk the boat, even though he was positive the boy was still tied to the tree. All those movies he had seen in which kids did terrible things just using their eyes. Well, Lippy hadn't really believed kids could be that spooky until today.

He looked down at the two plastic bags filled with money that he was holding and then at the bags Fingers held.

"If you hadn't sunk the kid's boat, we could have used that," Lippy said huskily. "Well, we're up the creek without a paddle now, partner, thanks to you."

"Shut up," Fingers said automatically. He was stunned. As vengeful thoughts ran through his mind, his eyes rested blankly on the pedal boat that the girls had used. Now, all at once, he really focused on it.

"Get in. We're taking that pedal boat."

"Me? Get in that? That's a toy boat for kids!"

"I said get in." Fingers' voice was hard. It didn't allow for any argument.

Fingers held the boat steady as Lippy

awkwardly climbed aboard and sank into one of the small seats.

"Where are we going to put the bags?" Lippy asked. "There's hardly enough room for my legs."

"If you were dead, you wouldn't know enough to lie down," Fingers snapped. "Don't you see how the boat is shaped? Like a swan? Hang one of the bags around the swan's neck."

Fingers tossed one of the money bags to Lippy, who did as he was told.

"Now hang the second bag on the other side."

"What are you going to do with your two bags?" Lippy asked. "There's no more room up front."

"It's a bird, isn't it? It's got wings, hasn't it?" If my hands weren't full, Fingers thought, I'd beat Lippy over the head. He stood in the water while he tied a bag to one wing and another bag to the other wing. Then, with great difficulty, he climbed into the boat and forced his legs into the narrow space in front of his seat.

"Hey! This is too much weight for this little boat. We could sink," Lippy cried out in alarm.

"Will you shut up and pedal?" Fingers roared. He began to pedal as hard as he could. Pushing down was difficult because his legs were too long. But releasing the pedals was worse, for then each bony knee in turn came up and smacked him in the chin.

Lippy was having a different problem. Each time his legs came up, they hit the small steering wheel. That jarred the boat and made the bags of money bounce. So Lippy had to grab at them constantly to keep them from sliding off the boat.

"Keep your hands on the steering wheel, you birdbrain," Fingers yelled each time this happened.

Lippy was pumping his legs up and down as quickly as he could. Fingers was pumping the pedals even harder, in spite of the fact that he kept wincing each time a knee cracked his now tender jaw. But Lippy still couldn't hold on to the steering wheel, so the boat kept spinning to one side.

"Hold on to the wheel! We're moving sideways. Don't stop! Pedal!"

"You know what?" Lippy snapped back, "I'm getting sick and tired of taking orders from you."

Back on the island, Jeff and the two girls had watched helplessly as the two men pushed off in the pedal boat. They were going to escape after all. But now Jeff and his cousins exchanged happy grins as they watched the boat move in a crazy zigzag across the water.

The voices of the two men floated back to them. In the quietness of the island, they could hear every word, every sound.

Crack! Bounce! Grab! Shout!

"They look so funny." Jo-Beth giggled.

Suddenly Jeff stopped smiling. He had a thought. In spite of the way it looked, it was possible that the robbers really might escape.

"Listen," he said. "We've got to stop them. We can't take a chance. They might still get away."

"How can we stop them?" Mary Rose wanted to know.

"We're just little kids and they've got the only boat, anyway," Jo-Beth added.

"No, they don't. I've still got *The Sea Horse*. I hid it when I landed. And old Hugo's here someplace, because the robbers sank his boat. Come on. We've got to get to the other end of the island."

"And then what?" Mary Rose demanded, not moving.

"*The Sea Horse* can go faster than a pedal boat. We'll beat them across and get the sheriff."

Jeff pulled his cap down, settling it firmly on his head, and started off.

"Do we have to?" Jo-Beth asked in a plaintive voice.

"We have to," Mary Rose said. "He's got the only boat. Wait for us," she called, and hurried after Jeff.

Jo-Beth trailed after them.

This was turning out to be the strangest day of her whole life.

•13•
The Voice from the Sky

At exactly the same time that Fingers and Lippy were gazing down at their rowboat, Hugo Axel was staring down at his boat, lying under the water at the other end of the island.

"I don't believe it," Hugo said to Gertrude, who had finally made her way back to her master. She gave him a sad, sympathetic look.

Hugo couldn't remember the last time he had been this angry. "First they break the lock. Then they turn on the switches. Then they dig holes. And now they've gone and sunk the *Islander*."

Gertrude uttered a soft whimper.

"Kids!" Hugo snapped. Nothing could convince him that this wasn't the work of irresponsible kids running loose on his island. "I'm a patient man," Hugo roared, "but I've had enough!"

He reached for the walkie-talkie he always carried clipped to his belt when he came to the island. Pulling out the antenna, he began to speak so rapidly that the person at the other end had to stop him and make him start again, slowly.

"What do you mean, 'vandals'?" the other man inquired.

"Listen, put Sheriff Hutch on. Oh. Is that you, George? You better get over to the island fast. There are vandals all over the place. A whole gang of them. I tell you, they're tearing the place up. You know what else they did? They scuttled the *Islander*. That's right. They sank her. I can't get off the island."

As Hugo was explaining matters to the sheriff, he noticed that Gertrude was dragging herself to her feet and looking down the path. It was a lot of trouble, but she even managed to call up a menacing growl from deep in her throat. Her hearing wasn't very good anymore, but she had caught the vibrations of pounding feet coming her way.

Hugo stopped talking and glanced in the same direction suspiciously. He braced himself. He wasn't armed, but he could take on a bunch of vandals . . .

Just then a breathless Jeff followed by two equally breathless girls burst into view. Hugo stared over their heads, waiting for the vandals to show up behind these small children.

"Mr. Axel," Jeff gasped, "you've got to get the sheriff. They're getting away."

"Don't I know you?" Hugo asked, staring at Jeff. "Aren't you the Post boy? What are you doing here? Are you in with those vandals? And girls too." He turned his head to look at Jo-Beth and Mary Rose. "You're never too small, are you? Coming here to my island to get into all kinds of mischief. Breaking locks and digging holes. Aren't there any decent kids left in this world?"

"Please," Jeff broke in desperately, "they're getting away. In the pedal boat."

"The rest of them? Well, those vandals won't get away from me. No, sir. Not on your life."

"What vandals?" Mary Rose was puzzled. "Jeff is talking about the bank robbers."

Hugo looked confused. "You mean you're all bank robbers, too? Well, that doesn't surprise me. Nothing surprises me anymore."

"No!" Jo-Beth shouted. "You don't understand."

She and her sister tried to explain. Jeff, seeing the caretaker's bewildered expression, decided he couldn't wait any longer. He grabbed the walkie-talkie.

"You give that back!" Hugo bellowed.

Jeff paid no attention. When the voice at the other end asked what was going on, Jeff said, very quickly, "Listen. Two bank robbers are escaping from the island in a pedal boat."

Sheriff Hutch asked a question.

"Yes. I'm Jeff Post. What? Yes. The One-tree girls are here too. Please, Sheriff. It's the truth. They'll get away with the money for sure if you don't stop them now."

Jeff listened. "I've got *The Sea Horse*. We can chase after them meanwhile . . ." Jeff listened again. "Yes, sir," he said finally, and handed the walkie-talkie back to Hugo.

Now it was Hugo's turn to listen. When he clipped the walkie-talkie back on his belt, he told the three children sternly, "We wait right here. The sheriff is going to head them off in the helicopter. And the deputy is using the motorboat. He's bringing your father," he said to the girls. "Who is hopping mad," he added, shaking his head.

Mary Rose and Jo-Beth exchanged worried looks. Hopping mad! That didn't sound too good.

"Come on," Jeff said, breaking into their thoughts. "The best place to watch is from the ferry landing." Off he went with the girls behind him and Hugo following, trying to make them come back. Even Gertrude was caught up in the excitement and trotted after the little procession.

"There it is!" Jeff said with glee as the sound of an engine filled the air.

"And here comes the boat with the deputy sheriff, and I guess the other man is your father," Hugo told the girls.

"Oh, boy. Now we're going to get it," Jo-Beth said in a low voice.

Fingers and Lippy, meanwhile, were pedaling away furiously.

"Where did the whirlybird come from?" Lippy gasped, looking up at the helicopter. A face peered down at them. Then a voice from the sky thundered down. It was Sheriff Hutch on the bullhorn: "You men turn around and go back to the island."

Fingers clutched the money. "Keep going," he told Lippy grimly.

But his partner knew it was all over. "They've got us," Lippy said. "We better do what they want."

By this time the motorboat had come close, rocking the pedal boat in its backwash.

Fingers looked up at the helicopter hovering overhead and then across to the boat. "I shouldn't have listened to you." His tiger

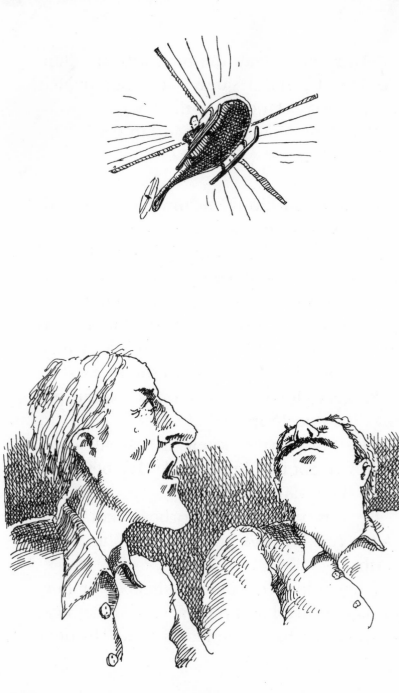

eyes seemed more yellow than before. "I should have gotten rid of the kid. Then none of this would have happened."

"You can't do anything to kids like that," Lippy told his partner seriously. He knew. He had seen all the movies. Nobody could stop these kids. "They have this strange power . . . "

Lippy stopped talking. Fingers was saying, very softly, "I'll show you power if I ever get you alone." He held the money bags tighter. "Pedal, stupid," Fingers added. "You heard what the man said."

At the ferry landing, Jeff and the girls cheered as the pedal boat turned and made its way back to the island.

Hugo was staring at the three small children in amazement. They had finally been able to explain everything that had happened since Jeff ran away from home. Hugo kept interrupting to say that he couldn't believe it. But he did now, watching the pedal boat come in. Bank robbers on Hugo Axel's island! What was the world coming to?

In the pedal boat, Lippy was thinking about Jeff. He was wondering how it must feel to have coal-black eyes without pupils and to know that you could do anything with them. If Lippy had that power, he'd make everyone disappear, including Fingers, *especially* Fingers.

•14•
Just Like
Everyone Else

Jeff and Mary Rose had expected to be
yelled at, Jeff for running away and Mary
Rose for not stopping him. It was certainly
plain to everyone that Mr. Onetree was, as
Hugo had warned, hopping mad. But Mr.
Onetree said not one word while they all
waited for everything to be sorted out. The
bank robbers wound up in the local jail.
Sheriff Hutch took charge of the money.
Hugo Axel was dropped off at his home.

Jo-Beth couldn't stand her father's silence. The least he could do was scold them,
she thought. It would be like a thunder-
storm, lots of noise and wild streaks of lightning. But then it would be over, the sun
would shine again and everybody would
feel lots better.

The three children piled into the Onetree car, Jeff in front with his uncle and the two girls in back. Jo-Beth was the first to notice that they weren't going back to Grandmother's house. "Daddy! Where are you taking us?"

Jeff turned pale. He eyed his uncle warily. He had never come across a grown-up before who didn't shout and carry on when he was angry. What terrible punishment was Uncle Harry planning?

The car came to a stop in the center of the small town, in front of a sign that hung from an iron bar: MAUD'S OLD-FASHIONED ICE CREAM PARLOUR AND EMPORIUM.

"Out!" Mr. Onetree said, speaking at last. The three children followed him into the store. The girls gazed about with interest. There were tiny round marble-topped tables and high-backed chairs with red-and-white seats. At the other end of the store, there were barrels and barrels of candy. The girls were amazed. They had never seen candy displayed this way before. Everything was marked plainly —

red licorice, black licorice, taffy, peanut brittle, chocolate bark. One barrel held odd-shaped crystal-like lumps of sugar with strings running through them. These were called rock candy.

The girls imagined that a rosy-cheeked, gray-haired grandmotherly old lady with merry brown eyes would take their order. Maud, however, turned out to be a small birdlike old man who held his head perkily to one side and didn't write anything down because, although he searched all his pockets, he couldn't find his pencil. Just the same, he brought them just what they ordered: Mary Rose a chocolate, banana and graham cracker soda; Jeff a strawberry, pistachio and marshmallow soda; Jo-Beth a cherry, coconut, fudge-twirl and peach soda; and Mr. Onetree a coffee ice cream soda.

When the last sucking sound through straws announced that the sodas were finished, Mr. Onetree sat back and regarded the children.

"I want you to know," he began quietly, "that I was absolutely furious with you, all of you. You gave me a very worrisome time."

Jeff looked down at the table and Mary Rose studied her hands as if she had never noticed them until just this moment. Jo-Beth started to say something, but her father shook his head.

"But once I knew you were all safe," Mr. Onetree went on, "I felt I ought to give you a fair chance to explain what happened and why it happened. Now, who wants to go first?"

"I guess I should, since I was the one that got this whole thing started," Jeff began reluctantly. He didn't leave anything out, including his anger at his grandmother for leaving. No one interrupted.

Then it was Mary Rose's turn. This time, however, Jo-Beth couldn't help interrupting. Between the two of them, they explained the day's events.

"I would say you've all had quite a few busy hours," Mr. Onetree said when the girls fell silent. He turned to his nephew.

"All right, Jeff. We've learned the how and the what. What I want to hear now is the why of it all."

Jeff was quiet so long that the girls thought he wasn't going to answer their father. At last, staring directly at his uncle, he said, "First my mom and dad went away and they never came back, even though they promised. Then Grandma went away this morning. And she said she was coming back. She promised too. But she won't. Grown-ups never keep their promises."

Mr. Onetree started to interrupt, then decided not to say anything. He just nodded his head to show Jeff that he was listening very closely.

"So then I figured you grown-ups would start wondering what to do with me. And I decided kids can't depend on grown-ups for anything. Anyway, I can take care of myself. So I just ran away. And that's it."

"But there was a reason why your mommy and daddy couldn't keep their promise," Mary Rose said. "It wasn't their fault!"

"They could have taken me with them," Jeff shouted at her.

"Then you'd be dead too!" Jo-Beth exclaimed.

Mary Rose was shocked. "That's a terrible thing to say."

"I don't care," Jeff insisted. "They shouldn't have gone — "

"Why not?" Mary Rose broke in impatiently. "They didn't *know* what was going to happen. Did you know what was going to happen to you when you went to the island? Of course not. When you make plans for something, you always think it's going to work out right. Isn't that so, Daddy? Otherwise, what would be the use of anyone ever making any plans?"

Jeff considered what Mary Rose had just said. Somehow things looked different seen through his cousin's eyes. He looked at her with new respect. Mary Rose was really a very smart girl.

"It would be very hard for all of us if we couldn't be positive about the plans we make, don't you think, Jeff?" His uncle put his arm around the boy's shoulder. "You know, Jeff," he went on, his voice low and gentle, "when your parents died, your grandmother lost her only son, and your aunt — "

"He means my mom," Jo-Beth interrupted.

" — your aunt lost a very dear sister. It's terrible to lose your parents, especially when you're still a very young child. But think about your grandmother. Can you imagine what her sorrow was like? Or how your aunt felt? And what she still feels?"

Jeff ran his finger around the rim of his glass. He didn't seem to be listening, but Mr. Onetree knew Jeff was absorbing every word.

"We all loved your father and mother very much. And we haven't forgotten them. We'll never forget them. But maybe after a while it won't hurt as much."

Jeff looked up at his uncle quickly, then stared down at the table. He knew the sadness he carried inside might never disappear. But now he understood that his grandmother and his aunt and uncle were hurting too. That helped — some.

"Shall we go?" Mr. Onetree asked, breaking into Jeff's thoughts.

"Just answer one question first, Daddy,"

Mary Rose said. She'd been curious ever since they had come to Maud's for their sodas. "How come you brought us here instead of punishing us?"

"When you're very angry the way I was, you say and do things . . . Well, let me put it this way: I knew I was too upset with all of you to listen to anything you had to say. I had the feeling you had all had a hard day, what with one thing and another . . . "

He's thinking about the Tunnel of Terror and those Dreadful Dragons, Jo-Beth told herself.

He's still mad about the way those men tied me up, Jeff thought.

He knew I was worried because he left me in charge and now he thinks I'm not responsible anymore, Mary Rose thought.

"We all needed a cooling-off period," Mr. Onetree went on. "And now we do have to go. I promised your mother," he told the girls, although he looked straight at Jeff as he spoke, "that we would get back home before dark."

"But, Daddy," Mary Rose told him, "we'll never make it home before dark now."

Jeff could feel his face getting red. It was his fault that his uncle had to break a promise.

"I'm awfully sorry, Uncle Harry."

"It's the way things go sometimes," his uncle answered. "Do you understand that now, Jeff?" When Jeff nodded, Mr. Onetree said briskly, "Okay, then. Let's go."

Jeff said impulsively, "Could I just call the hospital first and talk to Grandma? Just for a minute?"

Mr. Onetree dug into his pocket and handed Jeff some change. He didn't say anything then and didn't say anything when Jeff came back from the phone booth looking both relieved and happier.

"All right." Mr. Onetree started to stand up. "We're on our way."

Jo-Beth sighed. She hated leaving Maud's Old-Fashioned Ice Cream Parlour and Emporium. They didn't have anything like this back home.

"Could we have just one more soda? To share?" she pleaded. "One soda with three straws? Because we all had such a hard day?" she said pitifully.

Her father shook his head, then changed his mind. "Okay. But only if you race to see who drinks the fastest."

Jeff won easily and grinned at his two cousins triumphantly.

"I guess you do have the power," Mary Rose teased.

Jeff's grin grew wider.

"Why, Jeff," Jo-Beth cried, looking directly into his beaming eyes, "you do have pupils after all. Just like everyone else!"